10 LITTLE MONSTERS visit SAN FRANCISCO

RICK WALTON

ILLUSTRATIONS BY
JESS SMART SMILEY

FAMILIUS

GREETINGS FROM
SAN FRANCISCO
POST

To Robert Frost, who led us down
the road less traveled.

—RW

For 2005. Remember?

—JSS

Published by Familius™ LLC, www.familius.com

Familius books are available at special discounts for bulk purchases for sales promotions or for family
or corporate use. Special editions, including personalized covers, excerpts of existing books, or books
with corporate logos, can be created in large quantities for special needs. For more information, contact
Premium Sales at 559-876-2170 or email specialmarkets@familius.com.

Library of Congress Catalog-in-Publication Data
2015940073
ISBN 9781942672999

Printed in China

Book and jacket design by David Miles

10 9 8 7 6 5 4 3 2 1
First Edition

10 Little Monsters love to play
At the City by the Bay.

10 Little Monsters, they can't wait
To visit the city with the Golden Gate!

10 Little Monsters decide to come
To the Academy of Science planetarium.
One little monster points to the skies,
"That's my mom!" And off he flies.

The California Academy of Science is one of the largest natural history museums in the world. Its main exhibits include an aquarium, a rainforest, and a planetarium. You will probably not see your mom in the planetarium sky.

Lombard Street has eight sharp turns in one block. Drive down it slowly and pay close attention to the turns. If you have trouble with left and right, or if you're a kid, or a monster, you should let someone else drive.

9 Little Monsters, rolling so sweet,
Zig and zag down Lombard Street.
They laugh, they shout, with such delight.

But one turns left when he should have turned right.

8 Little Monsters plotting as
They take a tour of Alcatraz.
One says, "I'll escape today!"
So in he jumps and flushes away.

From 1934 to 1963, Alcatraz Island was home of a federal prison where some of the most notorious criminals in the country were kept because it was very hard to escape from. Unless you are a monster or a goldfish, toilets don't make good escape routes.

Ghirardelli Square is the home of the Ghirardelli Chocolate Company and a historic public square with lots of fine restaurants and shops. Everything tastes better dipped in chocolate . . . even monsters.

Ghirardelli

7

Little Monsters, at Ghirardelli Square,
See the delicious treats made there.
A little taste, so gooey, so sweet.
Someone invents a brand new treat!

Fisherman's Wharf is a popular destination for fishers and for tourists, which means, of course, great seafood restaurants. If you go, don't ask for the Monster Chowder. They are all out of monsters.

Little Monsters are in the mood
For Fisherman's Wharf's fantastic food.
"Here's mine!" says one, then he shouts it louder.
Now on the menu: Monster Chowder!

5 Little Monsters, at Pier 39,
Shop 'til they drop, then nap just fine.
Back come the sea lions. Look at that!

Up they plop and a monster goes flat.

4 Little Monsters travel down
A busy street in Chinatown.

But, oh no! It's a dragon attack!
One Little Monster never comes back.

3 Little Monsters want to ride
On a cable car, so they hop inside.

One finds a place where he can see well—
At least until they ring the bell.

Sit where the signs
tell you to, and hold
on, and you won't get
your bell rung.

2 Little Monsters curiously come
To explore the Exploratorium.
They discover. They play. They decide to invent.

One becomes an experiment!

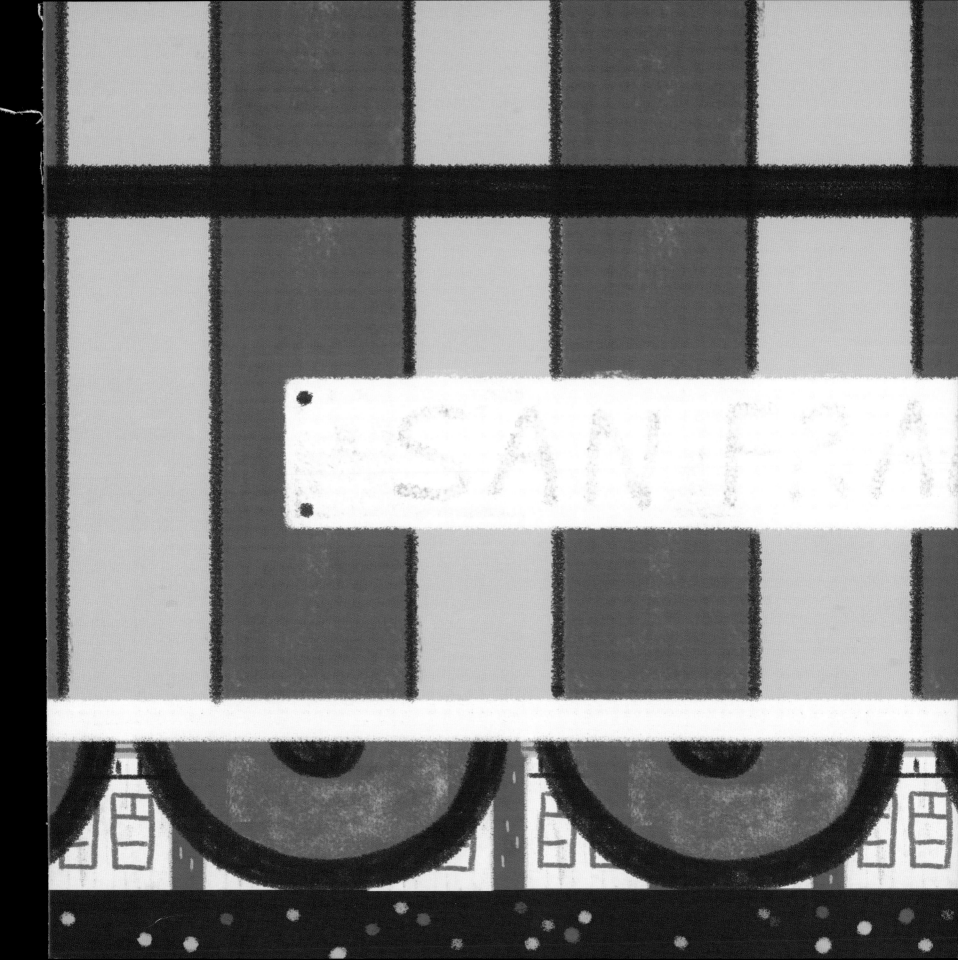

1 Little Monster, feeling great,
Walks across the Golden Gate.

The Golden Gate
Bridge is probably
the most famous
bridge in the world.
Little monsters
on big bridges
look like bugs to
seagulls. When
you walk across
the Golden Gate
Bridge, don't look
like a bug.

Down swoops a seagull from out of the sky.
There goes the monster.

Wave goodbye!